Morning on the Lake

For my son, Tom, who loves the northern bush.
And my family, who live there. — J.B.W.

To Ed, Mo and Herb, with heartfelt thanks. — K.R.

The Anishinawbe Ojibway words in the stories are *Mishomis*,
which means "Grandfather" and is pronounced *Mish-oomis*, and
Noshen, which means "Grandchild" and is pronounced *Noo-shenh*.

Text copyright © 1997 by Jan Bourdeau Waboose
Illustrations copyright © 1997 by Karen Reczuch

Published in Canada by:
Kids Can Press Ltd.
29 Birch Avenue
Toronto, ON M4V 1E2

Published in the U.S. by:
Kids Can Press Ltd.
85 River Rock Drive, Suite 202
Buffalo, NY 14207

The artwork in this book was rendered in graphite pencil,
Prismacolor and watercolor on Lanaquarelle paper.
Text was set in ITC Berkeley Oldstyle

Edited by Debbie Rogosin and Trudee Romanek
Designed by Karen Powers
Printed in Hong Kong by Wing King Tong Co. Ltd.

CM 97 0 9 8 7 6 5 4 3 2

Canadian Cataloguing in Publication Data

Waboose, Jan Bourdeau
Morning on the lake

ISBN 1-55074-373-2 (bound)
ISBN 1-55074-588-3 (pbk.)

I. Reczuch, Karen. II. Title.

PS8595.A26M67 1997   jC813'.54   C97-930588-8
PZ7.W32Mo 1997

Morning on the Lake

❖

Written by Jan Bourdeau Waboose

Illustrated by Karen Reczuch

Kids Can Press

Morning

"MORNING is calling. It is time."

I hear my grandfather's slow, quiet voice in the distance. There is no need for him to say it again. I jump out of bed, rub the sleep from my eyes and pull on my T-shirt and pants. As I run to the lake where he stands, waiting, I see his large silhouette against the pink morning sky. He is staring out at the cool, calm water. Morning mist looks like a gray blanket covering the lake. The sun is a big orange ball hiding behind the trees. I imagine it being pulled up by spiders' strings.

"I am ready, Mishomis." I yawn between the words and cover my mouth with my hand. I must be wide awake this morning.

Grandfather turns to me and smiles. He is wearing his favorite old straw hat. It has the feather of a hawk stuck in the band. I found it for him when we were walking through the bush.

On his feet are moccasins. Plain moccasins. No beads, no fur, no quills. He made them himself from moose hide. He made me a pair too, just like his.

Grandfather looks down at my feet, so I look down. I wiggle my bare toes. Grandfather slowly shakes his head from side to side. Then he grins. I grin too.

"Come, Noshen," he says in his gentle voice. He motions to the water's edge. His birchbark canoe is waiting there for us.

Long ago when I was little, I watched Grandfather make his canoe. He told me that when I was bigger I would make one just like his. I will too.

Grandfather stretches out his steady, strong arm. I hold onto it and climb into the canoe. It feels wobbly, so I sit very still. We begin to drift away from shore. Because I am in the front looking out, I cannot see my grandfather's face. But I know that he is smiling. I hear the dip of his paddle on the water and imagine many tiny bubbles trailing behind us on the glassy surface. I watch my reflection on the water as we glide.

It is still in the early morning. There is no wind and it feels cool and damp. Everything is silent, except for the sound of the paddle.

Grandfather stops the canoe in the center of the lake. He does not speak. This is his special place. Morning is his favorite time, and so it is mine.

We wait. We listen. We peer into the thin vapors lifting from the lake. It is so very quiet that I am afraid to breathe, for I do not want to disturb this tranquil wilderness that encircles us.

Then we hear it.

A low, mellow, haunting hoot echoing across the water. And then another call and another. I shiver, but I am not cold.

"Mishomis, did you hear that?" I try to whisper but I am not quiet enough. I see Grandfather raise his finger to his lips and then point. And I know that I must not speak again. But I cannot hold back my gasp.

There in front of us are four loons! A father and a mother with two fluffy gray babies on her back. The male loon moves closer to the canoe. He is not afraid. I wonder if I should be.

I can see the loon's white striped necklace. His shiny black back is decorated with white squares and dots. The loon is looking straight at Grandfather with his small red eyes. He stretches his silken neck up and then strikes his strong wings on the surface of the water. I feel the spray wet my shirt. I do not move as I watch the loon circle our canoe in a dance. Then, giving a sudden wild yodel, he dives with a powerful force.

My heart is pounding. I want to speak. But I dare not.

I know the loon has reminded us that the northern lake is his home. Grandfather has told me that our ancestors have given our people many stories of the Great Loon. This morning on the lake is our story.

I squint to catch a last glimpse of the family, but they have vanished. Gone, as quickly as they appeared.

The morning is no longer serene and still. Birds chirp their morning songs across the lake. I sense the animals stirring on the shore. The mist is gone. The sun, full and warm, shines bright above the trees. The wind ripples the water. The leaves sway gently in the scented breeze.

I feel that it would be all right to speak now, but I have silence on my tongue. No sound comes from the back of the canoe. I turn around to see Grandfather. He is smiling. I glance at my own reflection on the water. And I am smiling too. Just like Grandfather.

Noon

GRANDFATHER is looking up. I know he is searching the sky. Grandfather is wise and knows many things. He says I will too.

"When, Mishomis?" I ask.

"In time," he answers. "Wisdom will come."

I stand beside Grandfather. I look up and search too. The sun is low on the horizon. I feel the wind's wings, warm on my arms and legs.

Grandfather speaks softly. "It is time — we will go."

I want to jump up and down and make a lot of noise. But I do not. For where we are going only silence is needed. We leave before the sun climbs to the center of the sky.

I follow Grandfather like a shadow. Quietly, quickly, he moves like a fox, over the familiar path of the forest floor. I know that many animals have made this trail as they walked beneath the ancient white pines that whisper and past the singing water of the river.

But I don't see any of them today, only Grandfather ahead of me. I try to stay close behind, but it is not easy keeping up with his strong, silent strides. I stop a moment to taste a plump purple berry from a saskatoon bush and then hurry on.

I am hot and thirsty. There are beads of sweat on my nose. I am getting tired but I do not slow down.

Finally Grandfather stops. We are almost there. Almost. He turns to me and smiles. "You travel swiftly with soft steps. That is good. Now you must show strength as well."

He points to a rocky cliff and then tousles my hair with his long fingers. His dark brown eyes are bright and catch the sun's reflection.

"Are you ready, Noshen?"

I wipe the sweat from my nose, take a deep breath and nod.

"I am, Mishomis."

Before we begin our climb, I watch my grandfather's strong brown arms reach out and spread open to the turquoise sky. So I too stretch my arms high. Grandfather looks at me and nods.

As I climb, I can feel each rough groove etched in the face of the cliff. Its surface is hot and dry under my sweaty palms. My fingers are red and tingling, and I feel the hard ridges of rock pressing against my bare knees.

The cliff is steep, so I avoid looking down. Although I am not afraid, I am tiring. I keep up with Grandfather, but my legs feel as heavy as rocks. I cannot let this slow me, for I know that many ancestors have climbed here before me, and before Grandfather too. I imagine each foothold, formed through time by their steps.

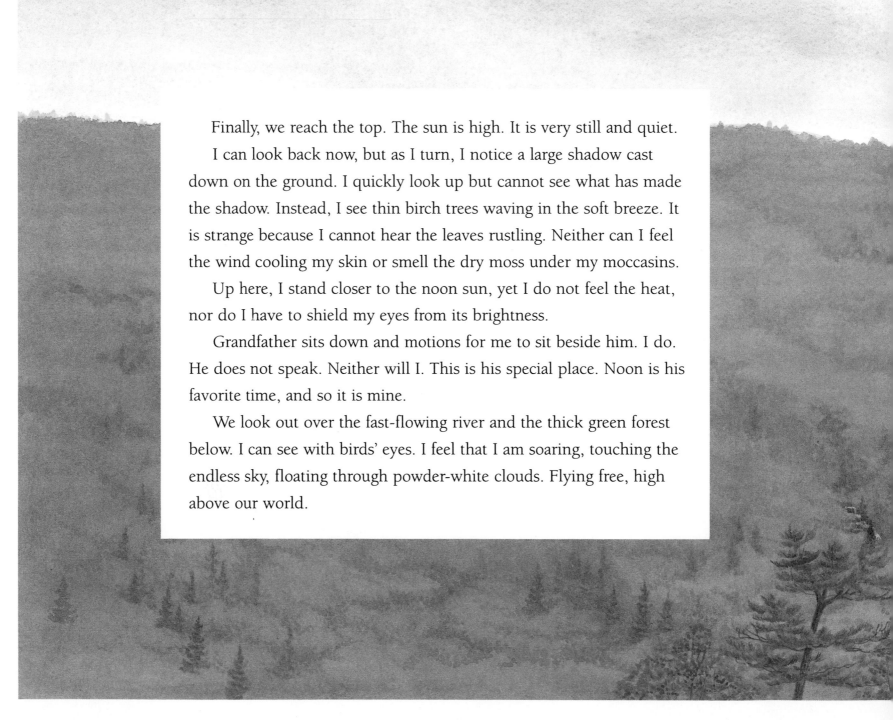

Finally, we reach the top. The sun is high. It is very still and quiet.

I can look back now, but as I turn, I notice a large shadow cast down on the ground. I quickly look up but cannot see what has made the shadow. Instead, I see thin birch trees waving in the soft breeze. It is strange because I cannot hear the leaves rustling. Neither can I feel the wind cooling my skin or smell the dry moss under my moccasins.

Up here, I stand closer to the noon sun, yet I do not feel the heat, nor do I have to shield my eyes from its brightness.

Grandfather sits down and motions for me to sit beside him. I do. He does not speak. Neither will I. This is his special place. Noon is his favorite time, and so it is mine.

We look out over the fast-flowing river and the thick green forest below. I can see with birds' eyes. I feel that I am soaring, touching the endless sky, floating through powder-white clouds. Flying free, high above our world.

Very still, we wait, perched on top of our rocky nest. I can hear my own breathing. It is loud. I cannot hear Grandfather's. I wonder if he is holding his breath. I want to look at him, take one quick peek. But then ... I see a powerful bird in slow motion. Alone and gliding.

In silence he moves with smooth graceful strokes. Around and around, he circles us with wings reaching like Mother's arms. Motionless, we watch.

The Great Eagle.

Suddenly, the eagle is looking at me. He is coming in my direction. Faster and closer he flies.

I do not move, not one part of my body. Oh, how I want to hold on to Grandfather. But I do not. My heart is pounding like the beat of the drum.

And then the eagle swoops down. I can hear the rapid rhythm of strong wings. I want to squeeze my eyes shut, but I keep them open, watching. He is here. His scent fills my nostrils. I feel talons combing through my hair with a gentleness I cannot explain.

Then he is gone, as swiftly as he appeared.

I let out a long breath and look at Grandfather. He is smiling, a very big smile. He points to the ground. There before us lies a long soft eagle feather.

I feel Grandfather's warm strong hands holding my shoulders as he speaks.

"Noshen, our people see the eagle as a powerful messenger. His presence is a sign of honor and wisdom. As the Great Eagle is a proud protector of our people, I am a proud Mishomis of my Noshen."

And so, I too am proud, just like Grandfather.

Night

It IS LATE, but I am not tired. Not tonight.

The bright moon is a huge pearled shell hanging in the night sky. A million stars like tiny fireflies light our way. It is quiet.

I point my chin up as far as I can and howl at the moon. The sound echoes back. Eyes wide, I scan the sky in the four directions. The warm evening breeze brushes my face like a moth's wings. It plays with my hair. As I walk, I feel the sweetgrass sweeping against my legs. My nostrils fill with its sweet odor. It is the same as the smell of the sweetgrass basket Grandfather made for me. I shall make one too, someday. But not tonight.

Grandfather's voice breaks the silence. "Have you found it yet?"

"Yes, I see it there." My arm shoots up, finger pointing high.

Grandfather chuckles. "Noshen, your finger could be pointing to a thousand stars, but there is only one North Star. When you spot the Big Dipper you'll always find the North Star. Remember this when you are in the woods."

We cross the open field and stand at the door of the forest. The tall dark shadows of the pines against the night sky look like animal shapes to me.

I have waited a long time for this. I have been in the bush with Grandfather many times, but not at night. I know that this is his special place. Night is his favorite time, and so it is mine.

Grandfather has told me that I must have the night eyes of an owl,
a nose as keen as a bear's and ears as sharp as a wolf's. I do. I am ready.

I can barely see his dark shadow entering the woods. Quickly, I follow.
I feel a strange chill beneath my jacket, but it is not cold. The air in the
forest is damp and smells of cedar roots, spruce needles and fishing worms.
The thick arms of the huge trees block out the moonlight. I try
to use my owl eyes, but they are not working very well. I feel the forest's
floor with my moccasins and lift my feet high with each step so I will not
stumble over fallen branches.

I cannot hold my silence and excitement any more. "Mishomis,"
I whisper, "when will we see the night animals? Where are they?"

He does not stop to answer, and his shadow in front of me moves
quickly. I imagine that Grandfather is a bear or a moose traveling these
woods in the dark. Yet he moves too swiftly and silently for either of these
large animals. I quicken my pace and follow close behind him.

Suddenly, a bone-chilling howl pierces the silence. I gasp and whirl
around. I am able to see now in the blackness. There are two yellow eyes,
staring, looking right at me. I hear the heavy panting of this night animal.

I am trembling. I try to turn in Grandfather's direction but cannot. My moccasins stick to the earth's floor like tree sap; they will not move. My arms feel pinned to my sides. But my owl eyes clearly see large yellow teeth, and I can smell the stale breath.

I want to shout out, *I don't want to be here.* But the words are not there. Neither is Grandfather.

So I speak without sound, *Mishomis, where are you? Can you not see me? Do you not hear this night animal? Mishomis, where are you?*

Then I hear his low familiar voice. "Noshen, do not move. Stay very still. The wolves will not harm you."

Wolves. I can't believe my ears. Is this really happening?

"Be brave. Show no fear. They mean you no harm. Stand very tall and straight and do not turn your back to them."

I can hardly hear Grandfather speaking. I try to be brave. Slowly, pulling my shoulders back I stretch my body as tall as I can. My eyes widen. There in front of me are several shaded figures, all with yellow eyes and yellow teeth, staring at me. A pack of timber wolves. The leader is still and erect, ears pricked forward, tail and head held high.

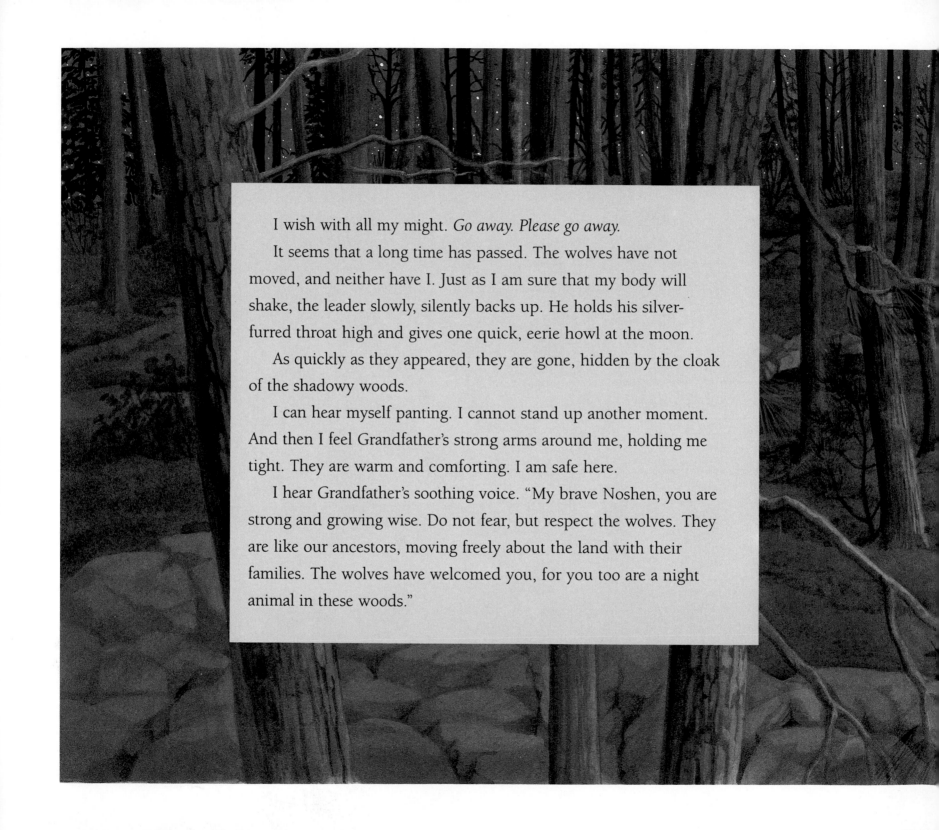

I wish with all my might. *Go away. Please go away.*

It seems that a long time has passed. The wolves have not moved, and neither have I. Just as I am sure that my body will shake, the leader slowly, silently backs up. He holds his silver-furred throat high and gives one quick, eerie howl at the moon.

As quickly as they appeared, they are gone, hidden by the cloak of the shadowy woods.

I can hear myself panting. I cannot stand up another moment. And then I feel Grandfather's strong arms around me, holding me tight. They are warm and comforting. I am safe here.

I hear Grandfather's soothing voice. "My brave Noshen, you are strong and growing wise. Do not fear, but respect the wolves. They are like our ancestors, moving freely about the land with their families. The wolves have welcomed you, for you too are a night animal in these woods."

I can barely keep my eyes open as I climb onto Grandfather's back
for the walk out of the forest. He moves as though I am not heavy, yet
I know I must be.

"Mishomis," I yawn. "Can we come back tomorrow night?"
I hear his chuckle trail across the open field of sweetgrass.